Ms Higgs Starts School

Story by Carmel Reilly

Illustrations by Beth Norling

Contents

Chapter 1

Monday Morning

It was Monday morning.
Ms Higgs got up at six o'clock,
because she didn't want to be late.

Ms Higgs was a new teacher.
This was her first day at school.
She was very happy,
but she was feeling a little bit scared, too.

Ms Higgs wanted to be a good teacher.
She hoped the children in her class
would like her.

And she hoped she would know what to do
if something went wrong.

By half-past seven,
Ms Higgs was on her way to school in a big bus.

Suddenly, the cars and other buses close by
started to slow down.
Then, some of them stopped.

"Oh, no!" said Ms Higgs.
She could see that a car not far ahead
had broken down.
"I can't be late on my first day," she cried.

Chapter 2

A Little Bit Late

It was half-past eight
when, at last, Ms Higgs got to the school gates.

There wasn't much time left
before classes were to begin.

As she hurried towards her classroom,
she dropped a bag.

Jack and his mother were walking past.

"Can we help?" asked Jack's mum.

"We can carry some of your things," said Jack.

"Thank you very much!" said Ms Higgs.

"It's my first day here,
and I'm a little bit late," Ms Higgs said,
when they got into the classroom.

"You will be all right," said Jack's mum,
as she walked around the room.

"Wow!" said Jack.
"Those are great pictures of rockets!
And look at the mobiles.
Who put them up there?"

"I came in over the holidays
to get everything ready," said Ms Higgs.

Just then, the first bell rang.

"I have to go to the office!" said Jack's mum.

She picked up her bag and rushed out the door.

Ms Higgs and Jack went out into the playground.

Jack showed Ms Higgs where the children

lined up for class.

Ms Higgs was happy to see Jack in her line.

She heard him talking to his friends.

"Our new teacher is great," he said.

Chapter 3
Where Is the Bag?

The children came quietly into the classroom and sat at their tables.

"Hello, everyone," said Ms Higgs with a big smile.
"My name is Ms Higgs,
and I'm new to this school."

As the children got out their pencils and books,
Ms Higgs picked up her bag,
to get her lesson plan.
"Oh, no!" she said, as she opened it.
"This isn't my bag. What am I going to do?"

Jack looked at the bag.
"It's my mum's bag," he said.
"She must have taken yours by mistake."

"All my lesson plans were in that bag,"
said Ms Higgs. She began to think quickly.

Then she said, "It's all right.
We can start with holiday news."

"I'll run and get your bag, Ms Higgs," said Jack.

"No, Jack," said Ms Higgs.
"You can't leave the school now."

"I won't have to," said Jack.
"My mum works in the school office."

Just then, there was a knock at the door.
Jack's mother came into the classroom.

"I'm sorry about your bag," she said to Ms Higgs.

"It made me think hard,"
Ms Higgs said, laughing.

"You will be a good teacher," said Jack's mum.

"Thank you," said Ms Higgs.